WAKE UP
OH! INDIAN
WAKE UP PLEASE

WAKE UP
OH! INDIAN
WAKE UP PLEASE

SUPRIO GHOSH

ZORBA BOOKS

ZORBA BOOKS

Publishing Services by Zorba Books, 2019

Website: www.zorbabooks.com
Email: info@zorbabooks.com

Copyright © **SUPRIO GHOSH**

ISBN : 978-93-88497-88-6
eBook ISBN: 978-93-88497-89-3

Zorba Books Pvt. Ltd.(opc)
Gurgaon, INDIA

DEDICATION

I dedicate this book to my parents Late Shri Bijoy Kumar Ghosh and Late Shrimati Monica Ghosh for their kind cooperation which helped me to create the contents of this book.

ACKNOWLEDGEMENTS

This book makes a small contribution towards awakening the requisite awareness level of the children of Mother India, so that they stop turning this beautiful land into a garbage dump. The chaotic reality of everyday, faced by the silent millions is slowly becoming the accepted norm. This silence is setting a dangerous precedent. Something has to be done to reverse the process and rectify the situation. To be able to do, what is urgently required, one has to be able to swallow one's pride & pretensions, and recognize the reality of our times, as it is.

I would like to thank many of the faceless millions who showered love and understanding on my arduous journey of creating the contents of this book. They are too many to be named here. In retrospect the list seems to be endless.

I would like to especially thank Dr. Eva and her colleagues at TPO and Delek Mcleodganj (Himachal Pradesh) for keeping me together (body, mind and soul) and for the reassurance through speechless routine actions that normalcy exists and is here to stay.

Suprio Ghosh

सचिव,
हिमाचल प्रदेश सरकार,
शिमला-171 002.

D.O.No.Spl.PS/Secy.-Edu./HP/2001.
Dated Shimla-2, the 3rd October, 2001.

The compilation of the poems by an angry Suprio Ghosh depicts the state of the nation of today. The poems reflect pain, despair and frustration that engulfs the common man due to the apathy and lack of governance on the part of the polity and bureaucray of India. yet it often ends with a ray of hope that things might improve with a little bit of sensitiveness on the part of those who matter. The frustration of the common man is evident when Ghosn writes.

> 'Plans and Projects are disastrous
> The results are everywhere to show
> If we don't plan properly
> How can we prosper and grow'.

The system needs to be revamped and this could only be done through conviction and commitment. Here Ghosh has a series of suggestions which provide solace to the reader that all is not lost. The optimist in Ghosh comes out in his words in a suitable tone of warning.

> 'It's time to act in a sane way
> and reap what we sow
> we must rectify our situation
> or the 'Atlantis Way well go'.

The poets concern is shared by many of us but unfortunately such concerns are not turned into action. The disenchantment gives way to frustration and cynicism and we drift with a callous and insensitive system. These simple poems can make one stop and think so as to reflect and realise what emnormous treasure we have within us. In the words of Tagore as rendered in English.

> 'When I go to Him abegging
> Whatever I get, I lose it again and again
> But when he comes to' me for alms
> I open myself to find enormous treasure within'.

Ghosh's poems may just bring about this paradigm shift in our thoughts and actions.

(Sudripto Roy)
I.A.S.
Commissioner-cum-Secretary(Education)
Govt. of Himachal Pradesh.

APOLOGIES

I sent copies of the manuscript of this book to the Late Shri Atal Bihari Vajpayee Ji when he was the Prime Minister of India and to Shri Lal Krishna Advani Ji when he was the Deputy Prime Minister of India for which I received letters from their respective offices appreciating my work.

Unfortunately overtime these have been misplaced.

Suprio Ghosh

CONTENTS

WAKE UP
OH! INDIAN
WAKE UP PLEASE

I WONDER

The Kargil issue has subsided
Will we remain as one?
Will we improve our lives?
Will cooperation be part of our fun?

Eradicating ignorance and poverty
Is what India needs today
Will our leaders be mature enough?
To bother, to show us the way

Will we ever be clean once again?
Dirty cities are all one sees
Community hygiene, we seem to have lost
We've to work together like bees

Come one, come all
We have lots of work to do
We've to rebuild this land
To bring happiness to me and you

We must understand 'Community Hygiene'
And grasp, what's civic sense?
We really must educate ourselves
To be normal with common sense

Work is worship
So we must do it well
Work brings prosperity and health
We must, the next generations tell

It's a sin to work halfheartedly
It's worse than work not done
It only creates complicated chaos
It's really beneficial to none

Filthy toilets and damaged roads
Haphazard constructions, bent electric poles
The infrastructure is breaking down
Cause our laws are full of loopholes

Chaos at the junction
Cause of no traffic sense
Ignorance is the root
It certainly is a menace

Garbage bins are not maintained
With litter, scattered all around
Civic sense we seem to have lost
Because most, to it, are blind

We must reeducate our people
The only way to achieve our goal
We must do it ourselves
Our efforts are required not dole

Will we remain as one?
To rebuild and fix our land
And maintain what we rebuild
To be proud of where we stand

A CALAMITY

Sit Indians and I'll
Tell you a sad tale
It'll leave you disappointed
Depressed enough to wail
The characters and situations new
Though the actions, very stale

The world did fret 'n' fume
When Pokhran 2 took place
They imposed plenty of sanctions
To stifle our growth our pace
They tried hard to eradicate progress
In our reality, time and space

They wanted us to suffer
Each one of us knew
Most of us read newspapers
Enough, to know it's true
And, experienced enough to understand
The foreign powers poisonous brew

It didn't bother most Indians
Cause they continued without shame
To loot 'n' plunder Mother India
Like wild beasts one can't tame
Rip 'n' strangle those who govern
For a pittance of personal gain

To handle this enormous calamity
At the international level
The government got hardly any time
Cause, like sponsored by the devil
Educated people were on strike
They knew not, blackmailing is not civil

The essential services sector
Went on shameless strikes
Blackmailing the government
For popularity and pay hikes
While the common citizen suffered
They screamed insane on mikes

Patients suffered a natural decay
Cause the medical staff were away
Teachers spewed poison
Teaching the young a selfish way
Adulterators and 'The opposition' went berserk
They decided to have a hay day

In this turmoil
Of multifarious dimensions
Where Indians weren't as one
Most with insane intentions
With a blind eye towards the enemy
Creating very unhealthy tensions

The chaos had almost
Got out of hand
But the forces of nature
Moved a magic wand
Many thanks to the almighty
Cause we are still a free land

But, this beautiful land
Is still by citizens raided
Public property lies damaged
Bent, broken or degraded
For avid shortsighted gains
Their souls, most have traded

No one complains
There is no one to care
The non-entities who notice
Are a rare fare
Unblemished careers are vital
There is none, who can dare

Who will bell the cat?
Do we need a stick?
Afraid of another emergency
It just might do the trick
We have to understand what democracy is
To rebuild brick by brick

Help me magic
Please help me again
Cause solutions are beyond
The human brain
Mother India is in turmoil
It's voiceless, in intense pain

AN URGENT REQUIREMENT

We must understand discipline
Understand the value of time
Run the nation with clockwork precision
If not, it's certainly a crime

We require discipline
To make everything clean
To imbibe civic sense
To make everything green

To be in time for work
To exhibit acceptable social behavior
We must incorporate it in our lives
It'll certainly be a savior

Clockwork precision is required
To be able to progress
At a steady pace
Without strain or stress

For that we should discipline ourselves
And understand the value of time
Understand the chaos delay causes
And how everything goes out of rhyme

How it burdens the treasury
Causes inconvenience to one and all
We must understand how it impedes progress
If not we are heading for a fall

WHAT'S ON?

Public property is damaged
Usually, before being completely built
It's, a common sight in our land
We accept it without guilt

Because we do nothing about it
Or, hang our heads in shame
We are just blind to it
Have our sensibilities gone maim?

The newspapers say nothing
No NGOs to make us sane
The politicians avoid the issue
Most citizens express no pain

Have we lost the desire for beauty?
Or, the desire, for pleasant surroundings?
Is the reason for this apathy?
No feelings for the nation, no bindings

Or have we become more selfish?
With no thought or care for the nation
Is integrity an alien concept for us?
We require healthy national integration

We are organized inside our homes
Clean, disciplined and caring
But the moment we step outside
Our discipline starts impairing

Somehow our values deteriorate
Somehow we lack commonsense
We litter and filthy uncaringly
Somehow we transform into a menace

We must reverse the situation
We can certainly, set it right
Cause most of us know what's better
It's just that we don't care to fight

Those who can afford it
Fly away to a beautiful environment
Not bothering, to mend their own
Turn it spick 'n' span like a cantonment

They don't realize
That we can fix up our land
Together, if we toil
We can make it really grand

30

HONOUR THE MARTYR

Clean up your motherland
For heaven's sake
What a beautiful land
Into a garbage dump we make
A bit of sanity and effort
Is all, it will take
It's a community effort
Each one's got a stake

Why not try?
To clean up our land
And really be proud
Of where we stand
Civic sense in citizens
Ought to be natural in our land
Compulsory education is required
And maybe, a whip in a hand

Degenerated minds
Who, couldn't care less
Urinate on street corners
Without feelings they mess
Creating disgust in others
Creating strain and stress
There ought to be strict laws
This calamity, a state of distress

Let's not mess the area
Around the garbage bin
It's an eyesore for all
It certainly is a sin
Medical problems are created
Emptying the treasury bin
Resources that could be used elsewhere
We need laws to eradicate this sin

Let's all work together
To eradicate this national shame
It's a part of our reality
It makes our progress lame
The problem is in the mind
Ignorance and apathy we must tame
We must impart awareness
Education is the name of the game

We must work together
To unravel the knot
Give everything to save the nation
As the martyr had sought
Progress is for certain
If we give, all we have got
To alter our present reality
We must sacrifice and toil a lot

CONTROL THE CALAMITY

Community hygiene has great powers
Brings pleasantness, soothes the eye
Beautiful cities 'n' country sides
We can achieve, if we really try

Our homes are clean, spotless
But our neighborhoods are filthy
That we don't protest is universal
Is the reason, callous apathy

This land of ours
Is passing through chaotic times
The result of our actions
Selfishness the root of our crimes

Against society
Against one and all
Let's correct our stance
Lest we, beyond cure, fall

The maintenance staff should understand
All dimensions of their work
They should function properly
At work they shouldn't shirk

They wanted the job
So they should do it well
On them depends the nation
To be healthy, clean and swell

We need a sense of belonging
To treat the nation as one's own
We need to alter our attitude
And transform, where the weed has grown

Let's become organized
And keep public property shining
We need strict laws to maintain
The environment, for which we are pining

Let's fix her up
And keep her clean
With a responsible staff
To maintain her sheen

One and all must contribute
Showing responsible behavior
We have to do it ourselves
There's no magic wand of a savior

A WAKE UP CALL

Public toilets are a disaster
How do we eradicate this shame?
People filthy facilities unashamedly
Is our education system lame?

Is self-respect missing?
Is there no sense of shame?
Have we lost our values?
Our sensibilities are surely maim

Most toilets are usually
In a disgustingly unhygienic state
Together we must correct it
This surely isn't our fate

Surely this is a passing phase
Till we educate our lot
Create a harmonious awareness level
And an urge to give others a thought

To feel for the nation
And keep it shining and clean
Emitting good vibrations
Maintaining a healthy sheen

Nothing is impossible
So this can be done
Let's relearn 'Community hygiene'
Unhealthy environments we should shun

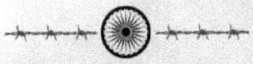

SANITARY EDUCATION AND ETC

Wake up Oh! Indian
We've to educate our lot
Community 'Hygiene 'n' civic sense'
The wise citizen sought

Though, chaos, through selfishness
Is, what most gained
It's a part of our reality
Rational humans, it pained

Oh! God help us
What a disgusting mess
What unbelievable toxins
We can do with less

It's poisoning the land
And hurting us all
Change is evident
Are we heading for a fall???

Teach us to use toilets & facilities
And not to misuse them shamelessly
And leave it as clean, as when in it one came
In the hour of need, not aimlessly

Leave it clean, for the next to use
So, the next doesn't feel disgruntled
Learning to respect others
May get us what's lacking and wanted

Oh! God teach us to use the toilet
Cause sane people, are there, but few
To leave it shining and clean
As though it were still new

Have we degenerated?
From a once clean race
Have we become so dumb?
And thick-skinned, a disgrace

Beautiful gardens 'n' community hygiene
Makes the land glow
But, maintenance is required
To give life to 'The show'

Educate your lot
And, 'The show' is born
Insane 'Graffiti' 'n' Scraped paint'
Is just 'Not on'

Teach them the desire
To live in beauty
Don't you really feel?
It's each one's duty

Mother India is our home
Home is not within some walls
That borders around the personal
Only not for 'Nature's calls'

And, all that rubbish
That each community dumps
Into the streets
Like from overworked pumps

Overflowing bins
And scattered plastic waste
Attract medical bills
At an unbelievable haste

Something Mother India
Can honestly ill afford
Wake up Oh! Indian
Or it's the end of the road

I'm sure we don't understand
What democracy means
It's not a way
To achieve selfish dreams

Freedom doesn't allow us
To lay the land waste
To mess up community property
To spread 'Bad taste'

Oh! Lord teach us
To be sane
Clean, healthy
And for none a bane

FILTER THE SYSTEM

The roads are full of potholes
The streetlights don't function
The signboards are disfigured
There's chaos at the junction

There's waste littered all around
There's filth all around the drain
They are transforming India into a dustbin
Their actions are totally insane

They keep their homes clean
And throw out the muck
Uncaring they filthy India
That's why we are all stuck

With gigantic disposal problems
Which our administration can't handle
And only excel in 'Passing the buck'
To somehow stay out of a scandal

They are there for their salaries
And not to do work
Any talk of responsibility
Their first reaction, shirk

Besides inadequate training
The will to do, isn't there
And, the problem is really compounded
By selfishness and lack of care

The system's got to be filtered
We've to try 'n' separate the muck
We can't afford incompetent officials
They burden the treasury buck

Besides the chaos they create
They are nothing but a national shame
Their morality totally degenerated
Young minds they poison and maim

To follow their footsteps
To rip-off without shame
No matter, who they hurt
Profit is the name of the game

We've got to stop this poison
It multiplies, everyday
I'm sure we can handle it
I'm sure there must be some way

If each citizen honestly
Dedicates Mother India some time
Imparting awareness in one's neighborhood
Will get things back into rhyme

The job is very tough
The disappointments are not few
But, one ought not give up
Even before the project is through

Psychological barriers are plenty
And opposition is not new
But, we've got to succeed
Even though we are only, a few

Sanity must spread around
We must help our neighbors grow
Time cures it all
Though initial progress is usually slow

Till that point of time
When things become a way of life
When progress is in leaps 'n' bounds
And life's without strain or strife

Let's filter our system
And sacrifice some personal time
To make Mother India beautiful again
Like a gorgeous maiden in her prime

THE TRAVELLER'S MALADY

No public toilets
On long highway stretches
And if there are some
They are in bits and pieces

They are never maintained
Causing inconvenience to one & all
The filth 'n' smell is so disgusting
People rather go to a wall

They destroy the surroundings
Cause, the toilets are blocked
It's so repulsive and disgusting
It leaves the tourist shocked

Most people misuse facilities
Most maintenance staff, don't work
It's high time, things became normal
The system needs a jerk

The people require education
Awareness about hygiene and diseases
About healthy civic behavior
About negative action and consequences

Facilities are misused shamelessly
Without caring for one and all
We certainly need lessons in using
Modern technology during nature's call

The people require education
The maintenance staff should work
They should be given training
From duties they shouldn't shirk

Understand the importance of their work
For which they willingly applied
Understand what's anti-national
It'll be a progressive stride

We must do something
To control this disaster
We must push the authorities
To function a lot faster

Tourism is good business
If the tourists come back
Can we ever achieve it?
If we, good facilities lack

IT'S HIGH TIME WE CHANGED

Filthy toilets
Blocked drains
Overflowing waste bins
Neglected pains

So much turmoil
What a chaotic mess
It overshadows joy
Brings strain and stress

We must do something about it
Cause this land belongs to you and me
There must be some way
To stop this deadly decaying spree

How to tell the people?
It's high time to end obsessions
Mother India wails and cries
She deserves care and concessions

NOT VERY LONG AGO

Once upon a time
Not very long ago
We finally achieved freedom
Independently, we could have a go

In managing our affairs
In rebuilding our land
But, we messed it up
Look, where we stand

Lopsided progress
Is a curse, for our nation
We should do something about it
We must cure our situation

Direction, discipline and determination
Should become our way of life
Only then can we survive
Through this strain, stress and strife

Consistency is what we need
Though it's tough to maintain
Even though one realizes, there is
Lots and lots to gain

How do we get out of this trap?
Is education the only answer?
Do we need a 'Social emergency'?
To quickly, get rid of this cancer

COME ONE COME ALL

We must cure Mother India
Our people have made her ill
We must all work towards it
And achieve our goal with will

Come one, come all
Help our land grow
We must help Mother India
And the whole world show

That we have social sense
That we care for our lot
That we have civic sense
'We are', what one 'n' all sought

Our cities, townships and country sides
With no waste littered streets
Where clean toilets and maintained parks
The visitor and traveller greets

Where people are friendly
And crime non-existent or low
Where helping is a way of life
With dignified charm in its show

Where people are just and kind
And, cheating a concept of the past
Where organized is the way of life
In its totality, till the very last

Only then it'll give meaning to
Our feelings of national respect 'n' pride
Who else, but the children of India
Can rebuild her with a disciplined stride

We must visualize our goals
And work towards them with will
We must make it a way of life
Awareness, we have to instill

Instill harmonious levels of
Community hygiene, civic sense and more
Guide ignorant fellow citizen
Towards a picturesque shore

59

LET'S TRY

Feel for the nation
Treat it as your own
Don't mercilessly deface and litter
De-weed, where the weed has grown

Don't misuse public property
Don't damage or destroy
A pleasant surrounding
Is for everyone a joy

Cleanliness is a must
So is beauty and grace
Only then we can claim to be
A civilized and cultured race

Let's fix up our nation
Find out where lie the errors
Who is responsible for this mess?
This chaos, this reality of horrors

Let's crucify the contractors
Who cheated to make money
Who have excellent projects on paper?
Though physically there aren't any

Usually a poor excuse exists
A fraud, a show, a front
Government treasuries are bled mercilessly
And we all face the brunt

Progress becomes stunted
And slow, in its pace
A few benefit monetarily
The rest, the music face

Let's crucify the education dept.
For the haphazard planning and it's result
For the apathetic attitude during work
Our state of awareness, an insult

The national average in civic sense
Is at an unbelievable low
Community hygiene is at a disastrous level
How can good citizen grow?

There is an epidemic
People are becoming more callous
More apathetic, more selfish
More egocentric and more jealous

Who is responsible?
For this bent of mind
We must detect
And, eventually, them grind

Replace them with a
More competent lot
To guide the nation
To achieve the change, one sought

Change is evident
Let's all do it together
Through thick and thin
Through good or bad weather

A wall is built
Brick by brick
Every effort donated
Will help, 'Do the trick'

WE CAN ACHIEVE IT

A flicker of hope
Turns into a ray
If we work towards it
Night and day
One, ought not stop
Come what may
Progress will for certain
Be there to stay

Leave the lazy attitude
There's lots of work to be done
Callousness one must leave behind
An apathetic attitude, one must shun
We will achieve a pleasant environment
And maintain the work that's done
The battle has just begun
A war has to be won

If cantonments can be spick 'n' span
Why can't the rest?
If we try to control this chaos
We can be with the best
Singapore has achieved it
Many more have passed the test
We must change attitudes and try
And toil towards a conquest

We can achieve our goal
And arrive at the desired shore
Well maintained pavements, meadows, roads
Organized, clean and more
This can be 'Paradise on earth'
If one feels for 'Beyond one's door'
We must build the crave for civilized living
And toil to be at the fore

We can achieve it
We must only try hard
Bad habits and negativity
We must with rationality, discard
If our strategy is correct
We'll emerge unscratched and unmarred
Into a pleasant reality
Which we ought to maintain and guard

WAKE UP

Awaken Oh! Child of nature
It's your mother who helps you survive
Don't misuse or waste her resources
Spread the awareness drive

Let's toil together
To cure our Mother land
Let's be firm with our values
Be aware of where we stand

Let's rectify the distortions
And resultant fallacy in our thinking
In our actions and lifestyles
Self or anything linking

Let's be harmonious with nature
Our beautiful Mother land
Let's maintain our surroundings
Let's make our environment grand

Let's inculcate civilized values
Become rational and sane
Kind and just in our interaction with others
And never, for civil beings a bane

Spread awareness and tolerance
So that we don't destroy
Make Mother Earth beautiful
For one and all a joy

The world has become a smaller place
We must understand the dimensions
Harmonious inter-action requires awareness
Prosperity and sane intentions

Each community must contribute
To rectify and rebuild its own
The mentality has to be altered
It's high time the seeds were sown

New education policies to change values
The mentality, lifestyles and more
And new laws to maintain policies
We will make it to the fore

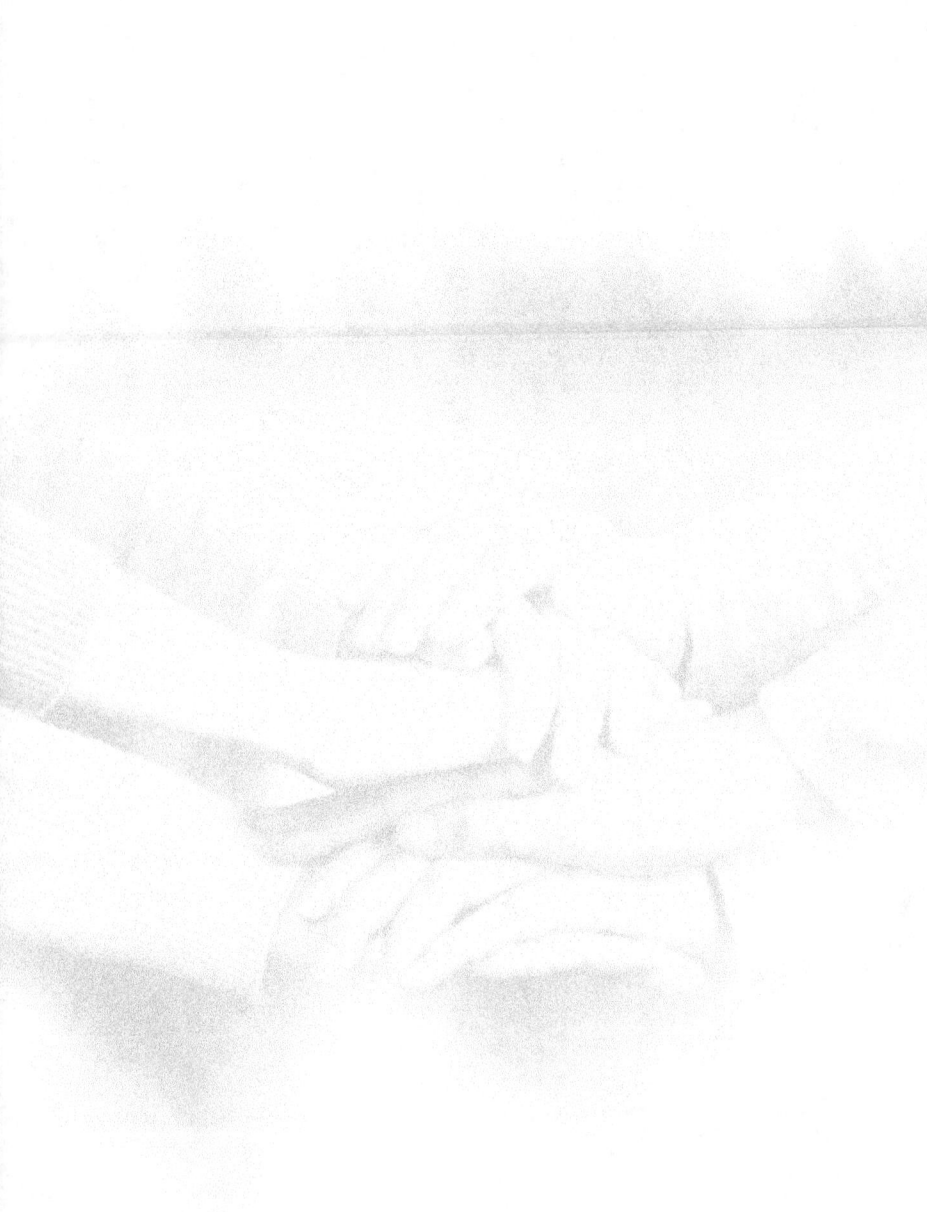

THERE'S LOTS TO BE DONE

Come one, come all
We've lots of work to do
With all our efforts
This land we must renew

Clean, green, pleasant surroundings
Is, what we need most today
To give our children the opportunity
The environment and a healthy way

To achieve this reality
We must rebuild and maintain
Or else, our resources will be
As usual, down the drain

It's high time we woke up
And reassessed, our situation
And restructured our institutions
To rebuild and maintain the nation

Every individual must contribute
The authorities can't do it alone
The 'I care attitude' must be imbibed
Every citizen contributing, one's own

'Sakshar Abhiyan' ought to be marketed better
Reaching out to one and all
'Civil education' should be compulsory learning
It's urgent, we ought not stall

Our society is a combination
Of a variety of mindset
We must have common goals
Or else we tend to forget

That this land belongs to
Each and every one of us
That each one ought to contribute
With pleasure and 'No fuss'

Let's roll up our sleeves
We must get down to work
We've lost enough time
We need eagerness, don't shirk

Cause pathetic maintenance levels
Is an eyesore for, one and all
Let's do something about it
It's urgent, we dare not stall

Let's make strict laws like Singapore
And make every citizen aware
Of heavy punishments for, filthy-ing and littering
So that no one will dare

Plans and projects are disastrous
The results are everywhere to show
If we don't plan properly
How can we prosper and grow?

Officials ought to be accountable
It ought to become the way
Inaction or wrong action appropriately dealt with
To maintain a progressive sway

We ought to become more organized
So that standards are maintained
The minimum, ought not become the maximum
Officials ought to be better trained

We need a bureau for ideas
Contributed by ordinary citizen
It's they who understand the problems
They face, daily by the dozen

We must learn to utilize potential
There is ample going waste
We must generate sources of income
If prosperity, we want to taste

We must build a work ethos
To be correct and precise in action
We must learn 'Healthy team spirit'
For progress and healthy interaction

Not just on paper
The results ought to show
If we go about it intelligently
Good citizen we can grow

Good citizen is what we need today
Citizen who are sane, responsible
Citizen who care for their land
We can make all this possible

REVAMP EDUCATION

The government tries its best
To spread adult education
To make us more aware
To strengthen our foundation

To make it easier for individuals
To integrate into society
Not be dependent on others
For functions of many a variety

But 'Sakshar Abhiyans' lie empty
With rarely a soul to learn
The project is failing to achieve
We don't have funds to burn

We must revamp the project
The advertisements are too few
The individuals who matter, rarely know
Or, convinced they can achieve it too

We must strengthen this area
So that illiterates come to learn
So, they can integrate better
With certainly more to earn

The curriculum ought to be broadened
Include community hygiene and civic sense
We have to achieve homogenous awareness
We have to cross this fence

Primary education is important
The government does a lot
But, the quality of output is pathetic
Is it lousy teachers, we've got?

Better training for teachers is required
To make them efficient during work
More interested and output oriented
The manpower requires a jerk

They build the pillars of our nation
Thus ought to act with responsibility
Not with disinterest, callousness
Since there is no accountability

Destroying the potential
At the roots
They are stunting our growth
They care 'Two hoots'

They just boss around the kids
Not showering love and care
They rarely explain the basics
So wide eyed the kids only stare

Without understanding what they read
The kids rote learn the whole
The end product is, 'The obvious'
There is rarely an efficient soul

The motivation is missing
Cause the teachers don't impart
Young minds with growth stunted
Due to, inadequate guidance at the start

Community hygiene and civic sense
Must be taught to one and all
Should be included in primary education
It's urgent, we ought not stall

The classrooms are overcrowded
No time for individual interaction
This creates minimal involvement
And lack of motivation and attraction

Killing potential success stories
Instead of helping their 'Growth'
Maiming potential good citizen
Who, frustrated, the reality loath

The bureaucrats justify on paper
The politicians use glib talk
But, the ground situation is deteriorating
And pathetic enough to shock

Statistics do not matter
If the situation is not improving
We have to correct the basics
To be progressive and moving

We have to solve this problem
It multiplies by monstrous proportions
Organize effectively with limited funds
Not apply, inefficiently conceived notions

If we revamp our system
We have a lot to gain
Our people will be progressive
Aware, wise and sane

NO OTHER WAY

We should really be serious about
Revamping the education system
It should become our priority
It should become our dictum

We should understand the reasons
Why we need this change
That we haven't done it as yet
Is shocking and really strange

Why are we so apathetic?
To this pathetic state of affairs
This ignorance, this inequality
This disparity, so obvious, it glares

This disparity creates problems
We should try to understand
We must eradicate it
And make the nation grand

It's creating inequality, disharmony
And chaos in our society
This lack of uniformity
Creates problems of many a variety

State run institutions, lack a lot
In infrastructure and quality of staff
Private institutions are unaffordable
Though their output, brightens the graph

Why can't we give?
The same quality
To one and all
To maintain equality

Giving opportunities to all
To have harmony in society
Spread awareness with love and care
To eradicate pains of many a variety

NO MORE HALFBAKED POLICIES PLEASE

Our policies are disastrous
The results clearly show
Inadequately researched and hastily conceived
How can progress grow?

The teams that assist the policy makers
Certainly need to change
Their attitude and eligibility questionable
Their awareness requires more range

Accountability should be a must
Cause since they have nothing at stake
Blindly they take decisions
And bad polices they make

If we need some examples
One can point at quite a few
That blunders are committed
Is not at all new

Blunders, blunders everywhere
No perfection in sight
That her sons and daughters don't care
Is the nation's plight

Hastily conceived policies
Waste efforts and resources
Depleting the treasury
Complex problems it enhances

Red-light areas are raided
To curb crime and free prostitutes
No rehabilitation, no relief
No psychiatric aid or vocational institutes

No specific policies to guide them
To achieve healthy social integration
Poverty forces them to retract
It's a matter of shame for the nation

The roads are full of potholes
Repairs and patches a common sight
It's because of superficial accountability
Bureaucracy, corruption we must fight

The documents show no discrepancy
Though the reality is a shame
No one complains about it
This attitude we have to tame

We have stringent standards
But, compliance, nowhere in sight
Half-baked policies to apply the norms
It's tragic and the nations plight

Shopping bags, containers and packaging are plastic
Though it's toxic everyone knows
Our policies encourage their usage
Though it causes environmental woes

Why can't we use jute?
Or some bio-degradable material
It's high time we used
Something that's with nature congenial

Instead of specified transparent bags
Less toxic in nature
Shouldn't adequate research be done?
To reverse this pathetic stature

Toothpaste, toffee, shampoos
Plastic packaging is used for everything
No toxic checks, inadequate research
Our policy makers, don't really care for anything

Our reality has plenty of examples
They glare, by the score
The govt. should no longer hibernate
Cause disaster lies at our door

They should study and understand issues
From each and every perspective
Evaluate and take wise decisions
With no personal incentive

With national benefits a priority
Sane decisions, should they take
With thorough research and responsibility
Wise policies, they should make

They should be held responsible
The accountability factor should be there
For creating chaos due to bad policies
This waste, strips the exchequer bare

We remain where we took off from
Stagnate more into chaos and decay
Complex problems arise, to create havoc
No more funds to save the day

We need better policies
Better utilization of meager resources
All actions and efforts, result oriented
And effective laws to fight corrupt forces

A MALICE

Bureaucracy and corruption
Are going hand in hand
As we are all aware
It's common in our land

'Envelope', 'Hafta', 'Ghoose'
Are, some of the names
This menace bleeds the nation
It stubs progress and maims

The financial state of affairs
And everything that's related
It mocks the terms, the rules
A new way of life is created

Where bribing becomes the only way
Or else the work is not done
One runs around in time-consuming circles
Maybe from father to son

Frustrating, irritating and expensive
Is the time-consuming affair
Most rather pay willingly
Of the hassles they want no share

India is a huge country
And most of us are poor
Ignorant about laws, procedures
Unaware with touts to lure

No information booths to guide them
No simple solutions and ways
Only red-tape and time-consuming paths
Frustrating and idiotic delays

Procedures should be simplified
No running from pillar to post
An efficient staff to handle affairs
Is what we need the most

It's about time
We found a cure
For this ailment of ours
This permanent festering sore

This life-style of bending rules
Promoting haphazard growth
The greed for illicit benefits
It's something one ought to loath

Punishments for indulging in corrupt deeds
For ones anti-national action
Punishments for bending the rules
Will certainly hinder the attraction

An efficient vigilance department
Uncorrupt and paving the way
Curbing corruption, cronyism, nepotism
Is, what we urgently need today

We've to discourage corrupt lifestyles
We have to change our ways
If we can curb this menace
We'll certainly see better days

UNAFFORDABLE JUSTICE

One can afford the law no more
Explained a friend the other day
Advocates hungry to make a big buck
And unfriendly policemen on the way

How the uneducated and poor survive?
Is baffling to one and all
For them I guess there is no justice
Cause they can't afford it at all

Most can't afford the system
Most don't have the time
Most have lost faith in its functioning
Be it civil, marital or crime

The wheels of justice
Move agonizingly slow
Creating a backlog
Blocking the flow

Years of hopes
And running around
Sometimes for a lifetime
There's no peace to be found

The judiciary is a failure
Justice is certainly rare
In time, without agonizing delays
Stripping the seeker bare

Law enforcement agencies
Are a pain in the neck
Something one would rather avoid
Cause the remaining tranquility they wreck

One has lost faith in the system
Cause cronyism & nepotism is prevalent today
It's time-consuming and agonizing
Cause of bureaucratic hurdles on the way

In practice the system is a failure
Some things have to change
It's not designed for one and all
It's unfriendly, incomprehensible and strange

Something has to change
Something has to be done
But, who will bell the cat?
When, to care, there are none

We need a new system
That's compatible to one and all
We feel unsafe and insecure
While the evil have a ball

Should justice not be?
Affordable and free for all
Justice should be equal for all beings
And be able to hear, each oppressed call

OUR REALITY OF EVERYDAY

It's a rip-off everywhere
The uneducated face the worst
Those who can't count beyond ten
Are, the one's to suffer first

The contractor, the shopkeeper, the moneylender
Exploit their ignorance and trust
Their children condemned to be uneducated
To satisfy the next generations lust

The conquerors have departed
But, yet we remain slaves
Is this what the martyrs fought for?
They twist and turn in their graves

Something has to be done
We must find a solution
It's high-time we started contributing
To rebuild and save the nation

Let's all wake up
And toil towards our goal
If we toil honestly
It'll bring peace to the martyr's soul

UNEMPLOYMENT AND ASSOCIATED PROBLEMS

No jobs in sight
For the educated ones
Unemployment is becoming an epidemic
Though there is hardly a dunce

Years of studies and hard work
Which parents could ill afford
Most with in-between jobs
No matter what they scored

Frustrated they sit in tea shops
Wondering what went wrong
Discussing, reality in canteens
They're sure 'Life's not a song'

Life's a mess they say
Due to political blunders
Disastrous policies, discrimination
'Crime and destruction' defenders

They are but pawns
They, for certain, do realize
In this game of chess
Of the sly in guise

It's a trap they don't like
That's obvious, for sure
They are just ripe enough
For crime and evil to lure

They are frustrated enough
To discard feelings for the nation
Harsh winds of reality
Causing directional aberration

This rapidly flowing brain-drain
The ever-rising crime graph
The deterioration of moral values
Mistreatment of the better half

Alignment with extreme elements
Anarchic philosophy, seeds of doom
This pressure, frustration and poverty
For sanity leaves no room

Misguided by propaganda
Brainwashed by mass views
They decide and act
It certainly makes sensational news

Infamous they become
They could have achieved fame
It's time to rectify policies
This situation we must tame

We have to consume our youth
Give them a positive direction
We have to use their potential
Their dedication in any action

Giving them the opportunity
To utilize their refined abilities
Giving them meaningful employment
Should be one of the nations priorities

The government must act
To expand the industrial base
Self-employment should be encouraged
If we want to win this race

THE AGONY OF THE 'CORNERED ONE'

In this chaos
This manmade mess
Stuck in this whirlpool
This strain and stress

Lost, without direction
Because all paths are blocked
No place for honesty
Leaves one disturbed and shocked

Days go by
And so do years
No openings, no anchors
To subdue ones fears

No openings, no paths
Shows, crime is the way
Though one plans to avoid it
Come what may

How does one cross this barrier?
Take a sane way
Honesty is unwanted
In this world of today

How to preserve ones sanity?
And avoid evil ways?
Love your fellow beings
Is what normalcy says

We are but human
With a stomach to feed
Crime is not necessarily
Done by people with greed

Want to avoid evil thoughts
It sucks one into its domain
How does one avoid evil?
And remain happy and sane

It's a turmoil one floats through
Trying to maintain direction
All is well that ends well
Oh! Lord, give us conviction

Give us sanity, courage
Rationality and strength
Determination and consistency
To go all the length

SEEDS OF DOOM

They rake old files
To divide us on communal lines
To ultimately gain power
And rule over us like divine

Distorting facts
To suit their tastes
Creating chaos, disaster
And inhuman wastes

Monstrous sub-cultures
They with motive, create
Using malicious propaganda
They breed fanaticism, violence and hate

They stub the growth of our nation
Our potential, our pace
Our positive attitude in life
Our compassion, our grace

They destroy our tolerant behavior
Our zest for harmonious living
Our ability to live happily together
Our peace and sense of giving

They exploit our ignorance
Our gullible and naive innocence
Mercilessly they manipulate
Deforming our attitude and commonsense

They turn us into monsters
Into thick skinned inhuman waste
They turn us into zombies
Its power they like to taste

We are a nation with diversity
We must realize
To maintain harmony in interaction
Is only sane and wise

Let's not fall prey to the manipulator
Let's shun him from our lives
We must eradicate this menace
Cause the nation for happiness strives

We are but human
We are apt to make mistakes
The efforts and will to rectify
Is all that it takes

To make our lives better
By not repeating the same
With willpower we will hold our direction
Consistency is the name of the game

Our reality will thus be different
Our lives productive and sane
Our actions will bring happiness to all
We all from it will gain

Let's try to achieve this
This reality, so near yet far
Let's live fulfilling lives
And heal every ugly scar

SELF-CENTERED CHILDREN

We invest in our children
To reap an educated lot
To bring progress into society
For a civil environment 'n' what not
To harvest a better future
What our martyrs fought for 'n' sought

But the cream, go far away
For prosperity, security and an easy way
Donating their intellect 'n' knowledge
Cause even second class citizen get a fat pay
Leaving Mother India to wither 'n' suffer
With a 'Who cares?' attitude, they go away

To lands far away
To work hard night and day
To prosper and to gain
To learn and follow the 'Normal way'
No matter how degrading
They claim to have a good day, everyday

But somehow when
They lived here
They deformed, destroyed and de-stabilized
Mother India without care
They had 'Uncles' for protection
Lawlessness, they did dare

They cheated at work
And anywhere else they could
They took pride in insane actions
Dishonesty was profitable 'n' good
That they are destroying their own
They never cared or understood

Now, when they come for holidays
They display flashy worldly ware
To the deprived in India
Who, can only gape 'n' stare
They criticize our total experience
And comment on the chaos here

Conveniently they forget
That they contributed a lot
Here they could have created
What every sane citizen sought
They would rather remain slaves
Who sold themselves or were they bought?

'Peanuts' is the price
Of a competent brain
Who, hover in poverty
With desires totally insane
Playboys, cigarettes and flashy goods
Temptation is really a bane

They don't send solutions
They couldn't care less
Maybe only some dollars
To relieve, personal family stress
They don't care for Mother India
They want nothing of its mess

They can go 'n' drown themselves
For all that I care
They don't respect their mother
Their ugly characters bare
We are better off without them
They never knew the term share

Truth and reality hurts
But no point of feeling low
I pray to you Oh! Almighty
Please help them eventually grow
Each one owes ones mother
Realization will help them know

DANGEROUS HOSPITALS

Public hospitals are all over our land
But they rarely bring relief
The public is usually frustrated
Lost, frightened and full of grief

Hospital waste is dangerous
But it seems we are not aware
It's dumped behind the rear boundary
There is no one to care

Flies feasting on it
Spread infection all around
Mongrels are attracted by the blood
Scatter it all over the ground

Public hospitals are filthy
The staff is just not bothered
The toilets are repulsive
The walls are usually smothered

They are only cleaned
Just before the CMO's inspection
They are not bothered about hygiene
No thought of infection, no introspection

Hospital waste spreads diseases
Our experts don't seem to care
It creates endless pains
It strips the exchequer bare

Hospital waste disposal
A reality, we can no longer ignore
A black mark on our claims to progress
A real challenge at our door

HELPLESS I WATCH

I sit helpless and watch
'Mother India' wail and cry
Cause nearly every place
Smells like a pig sty

Every place is full
Of pupils learning zero
There's rarely a place
Without a local hero

Who doesn't understand, civil sense
And disturbs one and all
Who doesn't care what he messes
While performing nature's call

Who lures young minds
Into certain disaster
To romp and profit
And remain their master

Showering indignation on the weaker sex
A vital part of their act
They have family protection
They know, its power is a fact

And there are more
Who think it's hep
To enact evil deeds
And that too with pep

So they dare to commit
Any repulsive, sickening crime
For them it's entertainment
A way to pass the time

Graduating from evil acts to crime
As the days go by slowly
He's really proud of his actions
He's never known what's holy

There ought to be some law
To eradicate this national pain
Occupation is good therapy
It makes one somewhat sane

Parents have rights
But, responsibilities too
I mean towards society
So...give them the shoe

A boot on their butt
They sure do deserve
And only with labor camps
Can, their children unnerve

It's high time they gave a hand
To rebuild our holy land
Something they mutilated
With an egocentric and avid stand

THE MENACE OF DOWRY

The menace of dowry
We've got to conquer and tame
So many campaigns against it
Yet all remains the same

Dowry deaths and harassment's
Are so common in the news
It's shocking and revolting for the sane
This black mark creates the blues

This anathema is a blot
Shames and degrades the nation
We need to reconsider our values
To achieve a healthy social situation

Social conditions
Are, a part of the play
Greed conquers one
Humanity lost the day

Shamelessly they demand
What they consider, their dreams
The brides' folks are mercilessly exploited
Their finances, bursting at the seams

Avid beyond imagination
For material gains
With glee they plunder
No matter, who it pains

Corruption is committed and justified
To somehow, cover the cost
The nation is bled once again
All moral and ethics are lost

They are mentally ill
That's for certain, for sure
They require assistance
They certainly need a cure

Marriage is, a union of love
It's never a business deal
By imposing unethical demands
The brides' happiness does one steal

It's all become so common
It's reached epidemic proportions
How do we get rid of?
This thick skinned lack of emotions

Forced upon, into a festive of love
Of romance, of commitments
Disfiguring and scarring the union, the bond
Is greed more powerful than sentiments???

We have to change certain values
For that we need strong conviction
We need commitment, belief in our abilities
Understand action and consequent direction

We have to change the mindset
We have to brainwash the lot
It's high time we achieved it
We have got to remove this blot

It breeds corruption
And the nation bleeds
How do we eradicate?
Such insensitive deeds

We need simpler procedures
And very strict laws
Quick and efficient justice
No loopholes and flaws

No mercy for the guilty
No room for parole
The media must play
A more aggressive role

In convincing the masses
To abhor, such inhuman disgrace
The mental makeup has to be altered
It's high time we transformed our race

It's a part of our reality
We can't deny the fact
If we want to eradicate it
It's now, we've got to act

IT'S NEVER ENOUGH

We come empty handed
We leave with pockets bare
Yet we accumulate avidly
Depriving others of their share

It's for our off springs
Some justify and say
Not understanding reality
That each has a different way

Time changes everything
Devouring all on the way
Nothing is permanent
The wise ones say

Fortunes are squandered
Before the third generation is through
They should have accumulated awareness
And not money, in my view

Money is means
To achieve an end
Though to get it usually
Rules are bent

Easy money is poison
It's very easily spent
Insane habits are accumulated
The character receives a dent

Maintaining the habits
Pulls everything down the drain
Obsessions rule each moment
Creating strife, stress and strain

Money ought to be utilized
Not misutilized, it is said
Use it to cultivate awareness
One will never be in the red

Money is important
Cause it makes the mare go
But character is more important
Let's together the world show

Let's spread the message
So that we achieve our goal
Every citizen ought to contribute
With one's heart, mind and soul

We who are fortunate
Let's show others the way
Our contribution will root out corruption
There is no other way

United we stand
Divided we fall
If this is true
We, ought not stall

Change is evident
Time changes all
Let's choose a sane direction
Lest we fall

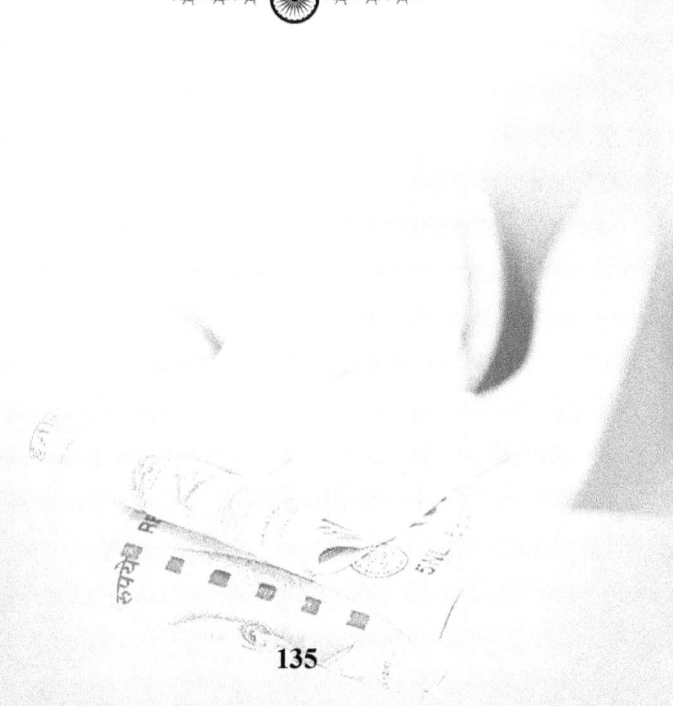

RESPECT FOR ALL BEINGS

Let's make sane laws
To protect one and all
All creatures, all beings
Or else, we are bound to fall

Love, hate, happiness and agony
All beings can certainly feel
It's a crime to ignore this reality
And become an insensitive heel

We know we are organic beings
And each one has a stomach to feed
To survive we can't eat stones
But, that doesn't justify a cruel deed

Shark fin soup one consumes with glee
But, if one knew how it's procured
One will lose ones appetite for days
And require a psychologist to be cured

Slaughter houses in most countries
Makes one's stomach churn
One realizes how sick man is
Horrid, selfish with an obsessive yearn

To display his destructive powers
To display his cruel ways
Oh! When will all this become the past?
Oh! When will we have better days?

We've got to eradicate
From its roots today
This mad mentality
Come what may

We've got to spread awareness
And brainwash the lot
We've got to spread love, kindness
Something all beings have sought

Let's inculcate mental attitudes
To respect one and all
Let's inculcate love and trust
Happiness we must reinstall

Transformation we ought to seek
To be able to do our best
To be able to do good deeds
Ignoring the past and the rest

Forgive and forget
Is the only way
To achieve happiness
And a better day

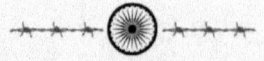

STRIPPING MOTHER EARTH BARE

Mother earth is in pain
The news and reviews, do show
It's high time we woke up
Or, the 'Atlantis Way', we'll go

Environmental degradation and waste mismanagement
Is, a reality of our times
It's destroying our Mother Earth
Future generations will pay for our crimes

Commercial viability
And massive gains
Makes no sense
If it other beings, pains

They save trees in their own lands
But, the 'Third World' they don't spare
They buy cheap with glee
While 'Mother Earth' they strip bare

Toxic waste is shipped
To lands far away
They don't pollute their own
Cause there they have to stay

They love their birds and bees
Their environment and the rest
Not caring for the rest of the world
They feel they deserve the best

The forests are full of living beings
Who suffer along with the trees
Man's destructive powers are beyond imagination
It brings all beings to their knees

Machines of war sow destruction
Innocent civilians suffer from its thirst
Though no one talks of the ecological disaster
And other beings who suffer the worst

Mother Earth can't bear the burden
We can't ignore this fact
It's already too late, but we must try
To handle the situation with tact

Soon there will be less drinking water
Many island nations will sink
Everything's disappearing at an alarming rate
It's time to stop and think

It's time to act in a sane way
And reap what we sow
We must rectify our situation
Or the 'Atlantis way' we'll go

THE CHOICE IS OURS

Heaven and hell
Both here on earth
We can transform our reality
And give our time, its worth

Our multifaceted society
With so much cultural diversity
Yet, united in the hour of need
Makes us a unique conceptual reality

We can be better than the rest
If we genuinely try
We have to get organized
We must modify and rectify

Team-spirit is required
To make things work
Let's all work together
Let's try not to shirk

Sharing ideas and problems
To achieve common goals
Let's fulfill the need of the hour
And not just depend on doles

We must compliment each other's work
And not stand against in competition
We must help each other grow
If we want to achieve perfection

A perfect society is utopian
But we can achieve the goal
All we have to do in action is
Put in one's heart, mind and soul

Impossible is a word used by
The ignorant, idiots and fools
Anything can be achieved in time
With the proper use of tools

Knowledge is the ultimate
Among all tools, they say
We who are fortunate enough
Should show others the way

Distribute knowledge
Let it spread
We must remain free
Slavery we dread

Let not the blood
Of the martyr go waste
If we make an honest effort
Progress we'll certainly taste

DO IT

Come fellow citizen
Let's rebuild this land
Let's be genuinely proud
Of where we stand
Certain aspects have to be rectified
We need every hand

We need everybody
Every heart, mind and soul
Every effort with an iron will
As we strive towards our goal
Thoughts, actions we must contribute
We ourselves must dole

Towards a perfect society
We ourselves, must comply
Only, if we make the effort
We will know the how 'n' why
We'll comprehend what's maintenance
And with a different attitude try

We must change this attitude
This state of mind
The 'Shrug', the, I don't care
To ones surrounding unkind
'Selfish', 'Callous', 'Apathetic' we must eradicate
And rectify all errors we find

Civic sense is a must
One and all should understand
In thought and action, it ought to be
Enforced with a disciplined stand
We have to maintain what we rebuild
Only then, our land will be grand

Learning about community hygiene 'n' civic sense
Should be compulsory for all
One and all ought to be aware of
Hygiene 'n' cleanliness during nature's call
Let's build and maintain an awareness level
This, we ought not stall

Let's make strict laws
To preserve civic sense
Attitudes will only change
If laws, are there to menace
Public property, ought not be damaged
And maintained, in a disciplined sense

Well maintained garbage bins
Pavements, roads and parks
No bills, no graffiti on the walls
No litter leaving ugly marks
Since a war has to be won
Willingly the sane embarks

STICK NO BILLS

To turn this land
Into a beautiful paradise again
The present state of affairs
Is for one and all a bane
Let's achieve what we ought to
Bearing silently all stress and strain

The blood of the martyr
Shall not be wasted
By people like us
Who freedom tasted
Cause then we will be
Forever detested

Must spread compassion
Love and care
Misuse is the worst
Let us all beware
And challenge all
Those who dare

To filthy and degrade
Our Mother Earth
She deserves tender care
Let's toil to maintain her worth
Every contribution is welcome
There's a gigantic dearth

AVOID SHIRK CULTURE

Don't be afraid
Of hard work
Don't be lazy
Don't ever shirk

Cause then one is chopping
One's own roots
Deterioration sets in
While one cares 'Two hoots'

Hard work is the only solution
To unwind the chaos everywhere
No amount of dole can make it work
If hard work isn't there

We mustn't be lazy
And shun hard work
We have to make it
We have no time to shirk

There is no substitution
Hard work is the only answer
If we want to cure the ills of our society
To get rid of the chaotic cancer

Work is worship
So they say
Let's work 'n' toil
Till we call it a day

That, awareness is bliss
One does slowly realize
Not a thing is achievable
Till one really tries

Success requires efforts
And a sane frame of mind
We must work hard to succeed
With no bones to grind

EACH ONE TEACH ONE

The pen is mightier than the sword
If only, the ignorant could read
If someone made the efforts to teach
It certainly, would be a good deed

Clarifying concepts and commonsense
Definitely isn't an easy job
Help build awareness to a harmonious level
Which exploitation, them, did rob

By shortsighted masters
For immediate gains
Leaving India disharmonious
And withering in pains

Those who govern us declared
Each One Teach One
It shouldn't remain a slogan
A war has to be won

Many battles have to be fought
The disappointments won't be few
But to succeed one must sacrifice
It's knowledge, that's not new

Donate some of your free time to Mother India
Some love, effort and skill
Be above petty politics and cooperate
Ignorance, we must kill

Teach them compassion
To read and to write
Teach them community hygiene
And that awareness is might

Teach them that cooperation
Is beneficial to one and all
Teach them that sacrificing
Will help us all 'Walk tall'

That knowledge is power
It helps avoid mishaps
We must spread it around
And help fill in the gaps

To eradicate ignorance
And associated pain and sorrow
We must all do it together
To have a better tomorrow

Teach them to make an extra effort
And to willingly donate some free time
We've to make Mother India healthy
We've to rearrange chaos into rhyme

We've to transform Mother India
Into an organized and a clean place
Where every citizen is prosperous
Where of disparity there is no trace

Where one is above petty politics
When it comes to a 'National cause'
Like eradicating communal disharmony
And hatred without a pause

We'll bring peace, harmony 'n' progress
We'll achieve it together as one
We'll make Mother India beautiful
This war has to be won

Each One Teach One
Should become a way of life
Don't let it remain a slogan
Let's incorporate it with an aggressive stride

TRANSFORM OH! INDIAN

Fifty years have gone by
And we are still lazy 'n' half asleep
There's no more time
To ponder astonished and weep

Its high-time we transformed
And made a clean sweep
It's obvious it'll take time
Cause the wounds are real and deep

Time cures all
So they say
Why not try
If, there is a way

We've got to make it
Come what may
It'll be a long walk
To see the light of the day

Wake up Oh! Indian
Oh! Wake up please
Since long lost you wander
Like sheep 'n' flock of geese

The reality's difficult to digest
It makes one wheeze 'n' sneeze
It's time to transform
Oh! Indian, wake up please

I sit and watch us
Half asleep, lazy and ill
And sometimes wonder
How? We are free and afloat still

We deprive our own
And subdue their will
To think beyond selfish ends
We've lots of poison to kill

We've to transform and grow
We really must rectify
We've to rebuild, reconstruct
And scientifically modify

We've to be sane 'n' rational
And curb the but, if & why
Or we'll certainly end up
In a monstrous pig sty

Poisonous ideologies
We've to keep at bay
Only then we will
Be able to walk all the way

Through the long, lonely night
Into a bright progressive day
We've got to make it
Come what may

We need introspection in certain values
We have to change our attitudes
We need to sort out our mess
We have co-related problems by multitudes

Inefficient administration
Blaring disparities
Barbaric law enforcement
Glaring illegalities

Ill-conceived policies
Gross mismanagement
Bungled projects
Perverse entertainment

Rising crime rate
Parallel economy
Imitation and piracy
Most pharmacies sell phony

Waste mismanagement
Medical problems
Financial bungling
Exchequer in doldrums

Inane competence levels
Viciously corrupted souls
Ego-centric, ego-maniacal
Motivation full of selfish holes

Disastrous, disaster management
Red taped bureaucracy
What a situation
Democracy or is it demo crazy?

Cheating the system
Cheating in the game
Attraction, compulsion, habituation
What a shame

What a shame
What a shame
Who's to blame?
Who's to blame???

Only promotions are important
And certificates to get work
The substance, rarely retained
Cause to understand, they shirk

Most teachers don't bother
They are too ill equipped, 'To care'
Knowledge is stuffed into kids
Not something, with love they share

Juggling innocent little flowers
The future of our land
Stifling, gold mines of potential
Destabilizing their stand

Turning them into wastrels
Liars, criminals and 'What not?'
Or far away from their goals
Nowhere near, what they sought

Too many to handle
Too disorganized is 'The show'
An amateur gardener
Can't make good apples grow

It's high time we woke up
And did something sane
To rectify and transform
This disastrous intellectual drain

Into citizen who care
Who respect and love their land
Who don't shirk or be ashamed
Of giving a helping hand

Who love their surroundings?
Their environment, their neighbors
And not into corrupt bureaucrats
Who, function only for favors

Please wake up Oh! Indian
It's time you moved your butt
Or we'll never get out
Of this quicksand like rut

It's high time you realized
This land is home to us all
And, build responsible citizen
Who, use the toilet for nature's call

And, leave it as clean
As when they had entered
And, not be unhygienic
And disgustingly self centered

Please wake up Oh! Indian
Open your selfish eye
Awareness, action is required
To answer the what, how & why

You have to help those who govern
To make uplift projects successful
And give a helping hand
To make Mother India beautiful

CITIZEN OF TOMORROW

Help the little flower
Help it grow well
It'll bring prosperity
I hear the future tell

I hear it'll bring happiness
And everything will be fine
It'll bring contentment and serenity
And values for which we pine

We must cultivate patience
Because, it's only a matter of time
Our nation will be a healthier place
It'll be, a saner place without crime

Let's not be selfish
And donate a few hours a week
Mother India is ailing
Her good health is what we seek

Let's donate positive energy
To help the little flower grow
If we work together as one
We'll reap what we sow

We'll be a happier nation
With a rational and harmonious vibe
Where corruption and crime do not exist
If we toil with a positive stride

Your mother needs help
Children keep her clean
The filthy environment makes her ill
It's only on you, she can lean

Cause on you depends, her hygiene
Her character and general health
Her reality, her state of affairs
Her prosperity and her wealth

ONCE UPON A TIME

Running away from 'Kal-yug'
I hit a lonely trail
There I met a hermit
Who seemed weak 'n' frail

Being a weary traveller
I decided to stop awhile
Soon I recognized his powers
And that he was really agile

He talked about the almighty
And about man and beast
He talked about greed and selfishness
And how people behave at a feast

How they overeat and talk big
Exaggerating in every way
How they shun and fear the normal
Their lives of everyday

Dissatisfied they are in every way
Cause they don't understand desire
Cause their only direction is money
But can't carry it to their pyre

He said one ought-not waste one's life
And do something for 'God'
For Mother Earth, for The Almighty
Eradicate wars, pain, and fraud

Poverty is a curse
It we must first eradicate
Ignorance, a poison
It breeds chaos and disgrace

We must awaken our people
Mother India is very ill
We must guide them to happiness
Love for the land, we must instill

I only spread the message
Of the voiceless Lord
I'm sure it will spread far 'n' wide
With the grace of God